First published in Great Britain 2003
by Egmont Books Limited
239 Kensington High Street, London W8 6SA
All Rights Reserved

Thomas the Tank Engine & Friends

A BRITT ALLCROFT COMPANY PRODUCTION

Based on The Railway Series by The Rev W Awdry

© Gullane (Thomas) LLC 2003

ISBN 1 4052 0695 0
10
Printed in Great Britain

TERENCE

Based on *The Railway Series* by the Rev. W. Awdry

Illustrations by
Robin Davies and Creative Design

EGMONT

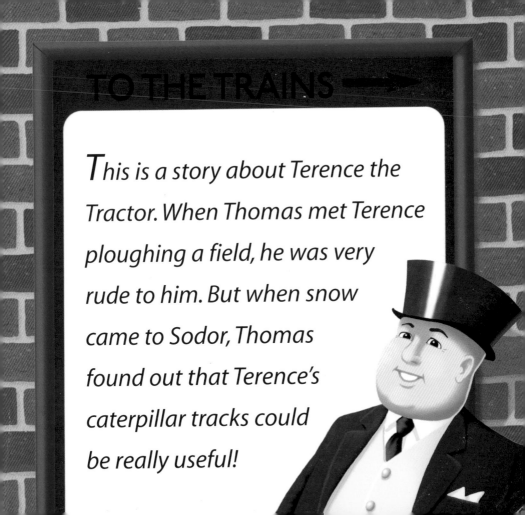

This is a story about Terence the Tractor. When Thomas met Terence ploughing a field, he was very rude to him. But when snow came to Sodor, Thomas found out that Terence's caterpillar tracks could be really useful!

Autumn had arrived on the Island of Sodor. The leaves were changing from green to brown, and the fields were changing, too – from yellow stubble to brown earth. As Thomas puffed along, he heard the 'chug chug chug' of a tractor at work, close by.

"Hello!" said Thomas to the tractor. "I'm Thomas. I'm pulling a train."

"Hello!" said the tractor. "My name's Terence. I'm ploughing."

"What ugly wheels you've got!" said Thomas.

"They're not ugly – they're called caterpillars," said Terence. "*I* can go anywhere. I don't need rails."

"I don't want to go just anywhere," replied Thomas, huffily. "I like my rails, thank you very much."

The next time Thomas saw Terence ploughing a field, he called out to him: "You've missed a bit – over there in the corner! Silly old tractor." And he whistled rudely.

Terence carried on ploughing and didn't reply.

Winter came, and with it, dark, heavy clouds full of snow. A snow plough was fixed to Thomas, but it was heavy and uncomfortable and he hated it. He shook it and banged it until it was so dented that eventually it had to be taken off.

"You're a very naughty engine!" said his Driver, as he shut the shed door that night.

The next morning, the Driver and Fireman worked hard to mend the snow plough, but they couldn't make it fit properly. So Thomas had to set out without it.

"I don't need that stupid old thing," he said to himself. "Snow is silly soft stuff. It won't stop me."

But as he rode along, the snow kept making his wheels spin and he found it quite a struggle. He passed Terence in a field. "You seem to be having some trouble there," called out Terence. "It's a pity you don't have caterpillars – then the snow wouldn't bother you!"

This time, it was Thomas who didn't reply.

"Silly soft stuff! Silly soft stuff!" puffed Thomas as he continued on his journey – and he rushed into a tunnel. At the other end, he saw a heap of snow fallen from the sides of the cutting.

"Stupid old snow," said Thomas, and charged it.

"Cinders and ashes!" said Thomas as he ground to a halt. "I'm stuck!"

And he was.

"Oh, my wheels and coupling rods!" said Thomas, sadly. "I shall have to stay here till I'm frozen." And he began to cry.

Just then, who should come chugging along, but Terence the Tractor.

"I heard you were in trouble," said Terence. "So I've come to help."

First, Terence pulled Annie and Clarabel away from the snow drift.

"Thank you, Terence. Thank you, Terence," they said. They were very relieved to be free of the snow, and were sorry that Thomas had been so rude to Terence.

Next, Terence came back for Thomas. He pulled and pulled, but Thomas was buried so deeply in the snow that Terence wasn't strong enough to move him.

"I shall never escape," thought Thomas sadly.

The Driver and Fireman tried to dig the snow away from Thomas; but as fast as they dug, more snow slipped down.

At last Thomas' wheels were clear. But they still spun helplessly when he tried to move.

Terence tugged and slipped, and slipped and tugged. And eventually, with the most enormous effort, he dragged Thomas clear of the snow and into the tunnel.

Thomas was very grateful. "Thank you, Terence," he said. "I think your caterpillars are splendid. I'm sorry I was so rude to you before."

"My caterpillars are certainly useful," said Terence. "But I can't go very fast. I couldn't pull a passenger train like you can, Thomas."

"Well, my wheels wouldn't be much use for ploughing a field!" replied Thomas.

And with that, Terence returned to his farm, while Thomas puffed tiredly back to the engine shed.

From then on, Terence and Thomas were good friends. Whenever they passed each other, they always exchanged a cheerful greeting – and they were never rude to each other again!

The Thomas Story Library is THE definitive collection of stories about Thomas and ALL his Friends.

5 more Thomas Story Library titles will be chuffing into your local bookshop in Summer 2006:

Fergus
Mighty Mac
Harvey
Rusty
Molly

And there are even more
Thomas Story Library books to follow later!
So go on, start your Thomas Story Library NOW!

A Fantastic Offer for Thomas the Tank Engine Fans!

STICK POUND COIN HERE

In every Thomas Story Library book like this one, you will find a special token. Collect 6 Thomas tokens and we will send you a brilliant Thomas poster, and a double-sided bedroom door hanger!

Simply tape a £1 coin in the space above, and fill out the form overleaf.

TO BE COMPLETED BY AN ADULT

To apply for this great offer, ask an adult to complete the coupon below
and send it with a pound coin and 6 tokens, to:
THOMAS OFFERS, PO BOX 715, HORSHAM RH12 5WG

☐ Please send a Thomas poster and door hanger. I enclose 6 tokens
plus a £1 coin. (Price includes P&P)

Fan's name..

Address..

....Postcode...........................

Date of birth..

Name of parent/guardian...

Signature of parent/guardian...

Please allow 28 days for delivery. Offer is only available while stocks last. We reserve the right to change
the terms of this offer at any time and we offer a 14 day money back guarantee. This does not affect your
statutory rights.

☐ Data Protection Act: If you do not wish to receive other similar offers from us or companies we
recommend, please tick this box. Offers apply to UK only.

Cut along the dotted line